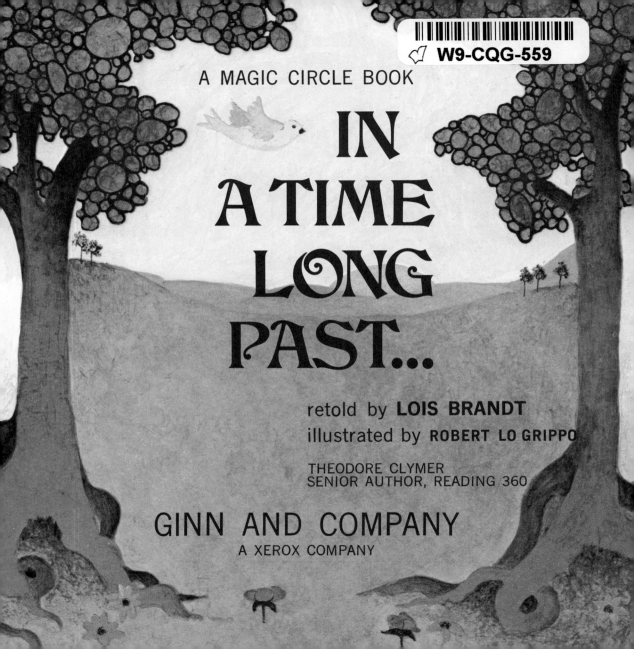

A MAGIC CIRCLE BOOK

IN A TIME LONG PAST...

retold by **LOIS BRANDT**

illustrated by **ROBERT LO GRIPPO**

THEODORE CLYMER
SENIOR AUTHOR, READING 360

GINN AND COMPANY
A XEROX COMPANY

Library of Congress Catalog Card Number: 79–157445

International Standard Book Number: 0-663-22987-1

In a time long past and almost forgotten, a woodcutter said to his wife, "Send Karla, our eldest daughter, into the forest with my lunch. I have much to do today and will not have time to come home. I shall mark the trees with my ax to show her the path to take."

When the sun was high, Karla started off, following the path her father had marked for her. She walked deeper and deeper into the forest, but not a sign of her father did she see — nor did she know that the markings on the trees had been changed by magic to lead her into the enchanted part of the forest.

By nightfall, Karla was hopelessly lost. Limbs creaked and leaves rustled in the night wind. Creatures scurried near her feet.

In the distance Karla saw a light glimmering through the trees. "Surely someone living there will give me a bed for the night," thought the frightened girl, and she made her way toward the light. When she came to a crude hut, she knocked timidly at the door. "Come in," called a deep, rough voice from inside. As Karla stepped into the room, she saw a huge black bear sitting at the table, holding his huge head with both paws. By the small stone fireplace lay three animals — a donkey, a fox, and a sheep.

Karla was terrified. But the bear said, "Do not be afraid. I will not harm you." Karla told him what had happened and begged for a place to spend the night. The bear turned to the animals near the fire and said,

"Dear old donkey,
Kind old fox,
And friendly, woolly sheep,
Shall we let our caller stay?
Do you answer aye or nay?"

"Barla Karla Koo-Ka-Poo," they answered as one, and that meant "Yes, Karla may stay." The bear said, "You may share our shelter and our food. Now cook us our supper."

Karla moved quickly to the fire and cooked a tasty meal. She served the bear and herself, but gave no thought and no food to the donkey, the fox, or the sheep. When Karla had finished eating, the three animals called out from the hearth,

"You have eaten of our food.
You have shelter for the night.
Sad times come to thoughtless ones.
Oh, you will prove us right!"

But the girl paid no heed. She turned to the bear and said, "The day has been long and I am tired. Will you tell me where I am to sleep?" The bear replied, "My bed is upstairs, and you may sleep there. I ask only that you leave the pillow outside the door, for I shall rest there and guard you."

Karla climbed the stairs and settled quickly into bed. She gave no thought to the bear's request and was soon fast asleep.

When the bear looked in from the doorway, he shook his head sadly at the sight of the thoughtless girl. Then he called on his magic powers. Three times he waved his left front paw and three times he said, "Dissa-Missa-Karla-Poof." Before he had uttered his last "Poof," Karla was taken by magic to an empty tower far from the hut in the forest.

Late that night when the woodcutter came home, he scolded his wife for not sending Karla with his lunch. "But, dear husband, our Karla did indeed start off with your lunch. Now I fear she is lost in the forest," wept his wife.

"Weep not, dear wife," said the woodcutter, "for surely she took a wrong turn. By now she has made her way to the home of another woodcutter. She is sure to come back tomorrow."

The next morning as the woodcutter prepared to go into the forest, he asked that Marla, their second daughter, bring him a jug of cool water in the heat of the day. "But I will mark the way more clearly so she cannot lose her way," he promised.

When the sun was overhead, Marla set out with a jug of water for her father. She followed his ax markings for a long way until the trail suddenly changed direction, and she wandered into the enchanted part of the forest. Though lost she continued on, trusting to chance. When night came, Marla saw a faint light and followed it to the hut.

She knocked at the door and heard a deep, growling voice say, "Come in."

When Marla overcame her fear, she explained that she was lost and asked for food and shelter.   Turning to the smaller animals, the bear asked,

"Dear old donkey,
Kind old fox,
And friendly, woolly sheep,
Shall we let our caller stay?
Do you answer aye or nay?"

"Barla Marla Koo-Ka-Poo," answered the animals as one. The bear growled, "You may share our shelter and our food. Now go to the fire and cook us our supper."

Marla cooked a fine meal and served it to the bear
and herself. But not one crumb did she give to the
donkey, the fox, or the sheep. When all was cleared
away, the three animals called out,

"You have eaten of our food.
You have shelter for the night.
Sad times come to thoughtless ones.
Oh, you will prove us right!"

"Hush, you silly animals," said thoughtless Marla,
"for I am tired and need to sleep. Oh, bear, tell me
where I will find a bed." Again the bear replied,
"My bed is upstairs, and you may sleep there. I ask
only that you leave the pillow outside the door, for
I shall rest there and guard you."

Without a backward glance or a polite "Good night," Marla climbed the stairs to the room. She threw herself upon the bed, and with no thought to the bear's request, fell into a deep sleep.

When the bear looked in at thoughtless Marla, he shook his head sadly. Again he called on his magic powers, waved his left front paw three times, and three times said, "Dissa-Missa-Marla-Poof." Before he had uttered his last "Poof," Marla was taken by magic to the tower where she joined her sister.

On the third morning the woodcutter said to his wife, "Be of good cheer, dear wife, and send Varla, our youngest daughter, with my dinner today. Surely she will follow the path and not get lost as her sisters did." The mother wept and said, "Varla is my dearest child, and I cannot bear to lose her." "Have no fear," he replied. "She is so kind and gentle that no harm will come to her. I will mark the way even more carefully with my ax and she will have no trouble finding me. By tomorrow our older daughters will have returned and we shall all be together again."

Alas, just as before, the ax markings led the girl into the enchanted part of the forest. When it grew dark she saw the light and came to the hut.

17

She asked politely to be allowed to spend the night there, and the bear once more asked the animals,

"Dear old donkey,
Kind old fox,
And friendly, woolly sheep,
Shall we let our caller stay?
Do you answer aye or nay?"

"Barla Varla Koo-Ka-Poo," they answered. And the bear said to Varla, "You may share our shelter and our food." Varla went to the animals and spoke kindly as she petted their heads and stroked their ears. When the bear growled, "Cook us our supper," Varla quickly prepared a meal which would please even a king.

When the feast was ready and the bear had motioned her to the table, Varla asked, "Are our friends by the fire not to eat? I cannot eat while they go hungry. We have food enough for all. Let them join us at the table." The bear smiled with pleasure and motioned the animals to join them.

After all had enjoyed the meal, the donkey, the fox, and the sheep called out together,

"You have eaten of our food.
You have shelter for the night.
Good times come to thoughtful ones.
And you will prove us right!"

The animals began to yawn and blink their eyes. "Is it time for all to go to bed?" Varla asked. "Would you please show me where I am to sleep?"

For the third time the bear replied, "My bed is upstairs, and you may sleep there. I ask only that you leave the pillow outside the door, for I shall rest there and guard you."

Varla climbed the stairs to the room and placed the pillow outside the door. To make certain of the bear's comfort, she took a cover from the bed and placed it, too, outside the door. Soon she was fast asleep.

At dawn Varla was awakened by frightening sounds. Howling winds rocked the hut and all within it. Cupboards slammed, doors flew off their hinges, and the chimney toppled to the ground. Beams creaked and crashed. In a blaze of lightning and a roar of thunder, the roof was swept away.

Varla huddled beneath the covers until all grew still. When at last she had the courage to look about, she found the room filled with warm sunlight. No longer was she in the hut — but in a great royal palace. The marble walls were hung with cloth of gold and silver.

Varla was lying in a queenly bed of ivory satin and overhead was a canopy of crimson velvet. At the foot of her bed lay a jeweled crown and a blue silk gown and dainty golden slippers.

At the doorway stood the bear. As Varla watched, he changed from a huge shaggy beast to a handsome young prince.

The prince smiled at her and said, "You have released me from the spell cast on me by a wicked witch. Until your kind deeds set me free, I was forced to live in the forest with only my three faithful servants to attend me. Your unkind sisters could not free me, so they must remain in the tower forever. But you, kind Varla, have broken the evil spell. Will you share my kingdom with me?"

Did the handsome prince and beautiful Varla marry? Oh, yes. And throughout the land, the people of the kingdom celebrated the wedding with music and dancing. And if they have not stopped, they are celebrating still.

24

ABCDEFGHIJK 7654321
PRINTED IN THE UNITED STATES OF AMERICA